GILBERT THE GREAT

Martin, forever in our hearts.
J.C.
For Chris, with thanks.
C.F.

The great white shark is one of the supreme predators of the ocean. White sharks can grow to about
6 metres, the females being a little bigger than the males, and can weigh over 3 tonnes. But, in spite of their size,
white sharks can leap clear out of the water!

White sharks are found in parts of the Pacific, Atlantic and Indian Oceans, and in the Mediterranean Sea.
Because of their rarity and secretive behaviour, there is much we do not know about great white sharks.

In warmer waters sharks are often accompanied by a small fish called a remora. Remoras can have
a close relationship with a shark, scavenging for leftover food and nibbling off shrimp-like parasites that grow
on the shark's body. The remora may stay with a single shark for a while, hitching a lift by sticking to the shark's
underside with a special sucker found on its head.

The Shark Trust is the conservation agency dedicated to the study, management and conservation of sharks.
To find out more about sharks, become a member, or adopt a shark like Gilbert simply visit www.sharktrust.org
or write to The Shark Trust, Rope Walk, Coxside, Plymouth PL4 0LF.

SIMON AND SCHUSTER
First published in Great Britain in 2005 by Simon & Schuster UK Ltd
Africa House, 64-78 Kingsway, London WC2B 6AH

This paperback edition first published in 2005

Book designed by Genevieve Webster
The text for this book is set in Adobe Caslon
The illustrations are rendered in watercolour and coloured pencil

ISBN-10: 0 689 86140 0
ISBN-13: 978 0 689 86140 6
Printed in China
5 7 9 10 8 6 4

GILBERT THE GREAT

by Jane Clarke

illustrated by Charles Fuge

SIMON AND SCHUSTER
London   New York   Sydney

*F*rom the time Gilbert the Great White Shark was a tiny pup, Raymond the Remora stuck to him like glue. Raymond was always on Gilbert's side.

When Gilbert was stuck in the seaweed,
Raymond untangled him.

When Gilbert got dirty, Raymond cleaned him up.

And when Gilbert lost his first row of teeth,
Raymond helped him collect them for the tooth fairy.

Gilbert and Raymond had lots of fun.
They loved to play finball, tide and seek,
and sardines. They played together, they ate
together, they slept together.

Then one day, Gilbert woke up and Raymond was gone.
"Muuuuum!" yelled Gilbert. "I can't find Raymond!"
Mrs Munch checked her son over carefully.
Then she put her fins around Gilbert and
hugged him tightly. "I'm afraid you're right,"
she said, "Raymond has gone."

"Raymond was my best friend," said Gilbert.
"Why did he have to go? It's not fair!"
"I guess Raymond just couldn't hold on any longer,"
said Mum. "Remoras can't stick around forever."

She kissed Gilbert on the snout.
"Go and play tide and seek with the pilot fish.
It will help take your mind off Raymond."
But Gilbert couldn't help thinking about Raymond.

"Perhaps Raymond will come back," Gilbert said.

"Raymond would come back if he could," said Mum, "but he can't. Let's go and watch the Baskingball. The Thrashing Threshers are playing the Tidal Tigers. Who do you want to win?"

Gilbert looked around. There were remoras everywhere, but none of them was Raymond. "I don't care!" he said, and he swam off before either side scored a Basker.

After the game, Mum took Gilbert to the coral reef to see the clown fish.

"It's my fault Raymond's gone," Gilbert snapped as they passed an eel.

"Last week I called him a sucker!"

Mrs Munch smiled. "Everyone falls out sometimes," she said.

"Raymond knew you loved him, and he loved you."

The next day at school, everyone was very kind to Gilbert. He was allowed to play on the sea saw for as long as he wanted. "Cheer up," said Mallet. "There are plenty more fish in the sea!" "There isn't another Raymond!" said Gilbert as he swished his tail and swam into the seaweed.

Gilbert was still skulking in the seaweed
when Mum came to collect him from school.
"It's not the same without Raymond," Gilbert said.
"I know," said Mum, "but Raymond wouldn't want you
to be unhappy, would he?"

"No," said Gilbert through a wobbly smile. "I was lucky that Raymond was my best friend." Gilbert gulped. "But I wish he was here now. I miss him so much!"
"Sometimes it helps to cry," said Mum.
Gilbert cried and cried and cried and his salty tears mingled with the deep dark ocean.

Mum took Gilbert gently by the fin and towed him into
shallow water. Rocked by the gentle waves, they gazed out
at the vast sandy seashore and the endless blue sky.
"I hope Raymond's happy, wherever he is," said Gilbert.
"I'm sure he is," said Mum.

"I'm hungry," said Gilbert.

"We'll go to the Wreck," said Mum.

Gilbert's eyes lit up. They didn't usually go to the Wreck.

Mum didn't like him eating junk food.

Scrunch…munch…crunch!
As Gilbert was tucking into a pile of
tin cans and bits of old boat, he spotted
a small remora lurking in the shadows.
Gilbert stopped crunching and swam
towards her. Rita was crying as if
her heart would break.

"What's the matter?" Gilbert asked.

"It's my shark, Daffiny," Rita sobbed. "She's gone!"

"So's Raymond, my remora," said Gilbert sadly.
"But he's stuck in my heart. I shall never lose him there."

"Daffiny's in my heart, too." Rita smiled a wobbly smile.

Gilbert took Rita's fin and together they
swam out of the shadows.

A ray of sunlight filtered through the deep blue ocean. Gilbert's teeth flashed as he grinned a huge grin. "Would you like to stick around with me, Rita?"

Sunlight danced in Rita's eyes. "I'd love to stick around with you," she said.

*F*in